DINNER AT Joey's

Written and Illustrated by
Jennifer King

Dinner's as boring as boring can be . . .

But what if the dog ate his supper with me?
If the dog ate his dinner sitting here in this chair,
He'd slop it all over but I wouldn't care.
A dog at the table, whadda ya think about that?

Hey, while I'm at it how 'bout adding a cat?

Not a plain fluffy housecat, cute, fuzzy and sweet.
No, the King of the Jungle would join us to eat.

And how 'bout a tiger? The cat with the stripes.
I sure hope there's meat on the menu tonight!

And here comes a boa, who swallows food whole,
In struts a toucan whose beak's in a bowl.

Tucked in its shell
    the turtle eats in the dark,
        While up in that seat jumps a furry aardvark.
            A big dish of ants sits in front of his face.
                Ants? I don't think so—I don't want a taste.

In flies an owl, who grabs meals while in flight.
I can flick off the lights and pretend that it's night.
Hey now, what's this? Could that be a bear?
A wild, wooly, white one walked in over there.
He's next to the walrus, 'cause they both eat fish.
Fishsticks and flounder and eels on their dish.

In swings a gibbon, here's a slow-moving sloth,
A lemur, a gecko, a few fluttering moths.
The bison arrives and starts feeding his face . . .

Uh-oh!
It's crowded—we've run out of space!

My napkin is missing, my fork's on the floor,
The lion won't stop with that ear-pounding roar.
Dinner was boring, but now it's a zoo . . .
Shhhh . . . I hear MOM! All you animals SHOO!

She hates having even my dog in the room!
You guys have to leave!
And you have to leave soon!

Uh-oh it's her, and she doesn't look pleased.
Darn, she said I'd better finish these peas.

Dinner's *still* boring as boring can be,

But tomorrow it's breakfast for T-Rex and me!